ROGER LELOUP

THE ADVENTURES OF YOKO, VIC & PAUL

Graphic Novels

SCIENCE FICTION COLLECTION
The Adventures of Yoko, Vic & Paul

Vulcan's Forge
ISBN 0-87416-065-0

Written and illustrated by Roger Leloup
Translated by Jean Jacques Surbeck
Edited by Bernd Metz

Published by Catalan Communications
43 East 19th Street
New York, NY 10003

First Comcat Comics Edition, February 1989
10 9 8 7 6 5 4 3 2 1
Dep. L. B. 46276/88
Printed in Catalonia (Spain)

ROGER LELOUP

THE ADVENTURES OF YOKO, VIC & PAUL

1 VULCAN'S FORGE

catalan communications
new york

ONE EVENING...
HOME AT LAST! WORKING FOR TV IS EXHAUSTING!... AND YET...

...I'M JUST AS HOOKED ON IT AS EVERYONE ELSE... THERE'S A GOOD MOVIE AFTER THE NEWS... JUST ENOUGH TIME TO MAKE A GOOD CUP OF TEA!

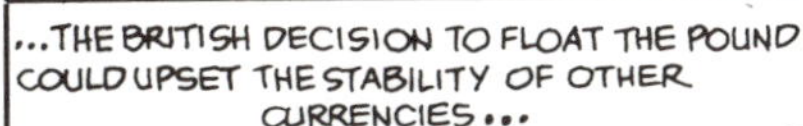
...THE BRITISH DECISION TO FLOAT THE POUND COULD UPSET THE STABILITY OF OTHER CURRENCIES...

AS LONG AS THEY DON'T TOUCH THE YEN, MY SAVINGS ARE OK!

THIS JUST IN: AN UNKNOWN ELEMENT SEEMS TO HAVE BEEN DISCOVERED IN THE CARIBBEAN...
?

...OFF THE COAST OF MARTINIQUE, AN OIL RIG DRILLING OFF SHORE HIT THE HARDEST SUBSTANCE EVER ENCOUNTERED, BREAKING THE DRILL BIT. RECOVERED FRAGMENTS ARE DESCRIBED AS GLAZED, LUMINOUS AND HIGHLY MAGNETIC...

...IN FACT, THE ENTIRE RIG BECAME MAGNETIZED...

OH NO! I DON'T BELIEVE IT!

GLAZED!...

...LUMINOUS!...

...MAGNETIC!... GOT TO CALL PAUL!

THAT'S IT FOR THE NEWS. RECAPPING THE HEADLINES...

BUSY!... HE'S HOME!... I'LL DRIVE OVER!...
BEEP-BEEP-BEEP...

MEANWHILE, AT THE OTHER END...
DARN!! BUSY!... IF SHE'S ON THE PHONE, SHE MISSED THE NEWS!... GOT TO RUN TO HER PLACE!...
BEEP-BEEP-BEEP...
HEADLINES...

5 MINUTES LATER...
GREAT TIME TO TRY OUT MY NEW TOY!
VROOP

ON THE AVENUE...
VROM
PHEW! THESE FUMES!... I'LL TAKE THE SHORTCUT PAUL USES WHEN HE COMES OVER!...
VROAP

RADIO-HOME
IT'S A DETOUR, BUT AT LEAST I CAN BREATHE!

HERE WE GO! NOW TO THE RIGHT!...
VROP

HONDA

YOKO!
PAUL!
VROOOMMM
BAM

MY BIKE!

OUCH! THE SPHERE!
PLAF
POF

POK

YOKO?!!... ARE YOU HURT?...
NOT A SCRATCH!... PRAY THAT MY BIKE DOESN'T HAVE ANY EITHER!...

THEEEERE!... IT'S PERFECTLY OK, SEE?...
GOOD! COME HERE!...
HONDA

HEY, THAT'S THE VINANS' SPHERE!
RIGHT! HELP ME GET IT OFF THIS TRASH CAN!

SO?... THEN YOU SAW THE NEWS!... AND YOU... WERE COMING...
... ONLY I HOLD MY RIGHT WHEN I TURN!... HOLD ON!... HUH!

HEY!

KLONK
3A

YUCK!

I DIDN'T REALIZE THIS BALL COULD BE SO DUMB!
ITS ENERGY ESCAPES AT THE SLIGHTEST SHOCK!

FORTUNATELY, THE STREET WAS EMPTY AND NOBODY NOTICED A THING! WHEN YOU'VE CLEANED UP, LET'S HURRY OVER TO VIC!
OH, NO! SHE HAS HER DETERMINED LOOK!...

LATER, AT VIC'S...
GO TO MARTINIQUE?!! ARE YOU KIDDING, YOKO!!...
MCX 488

TRAVEL 5000 MILES TO PROVE THAT THIS UNKNOWN MATERIAL IS THE SAME AS THE SPHERE?... WHAT FOR?
TO MEET AGAIN WITH THOSE WHO GAVE IT TO US!...
3B

REMEMBER WHAT KANI SAID WHEN SHE GAVE US THIS SPHERE?...
YOKO! TAKE THIS SPHERE! I CAN INFLUENCE IT FROM A DISTANCE... IT WILL TURN OPAQUE WHEN WE ARE RID OF THE ELEMENT IN OUR AIR WHICH IS NOXIOUS TO US... THEN, MY FRIENDS, COME BACK TO VISIT US!
THAT'S A PROMISE, KANI!

RIGHT! IT NEVER TURNED OPAQUE!
ON THE CONTRARY! ITS ENERGY AND LIGHT HAVE INCREASED!
TO GO BACK TO THE VINANS, ALL WE NEED IS TO GO THROUGH THE SIPHON IN THE CAVE!...

THEY MUST HAVE CONDEMNED THAT ENTRANCE. IT WAS TOO DANGEROUS... MY INTUITION TELLS ME THAT THE TECHNICIANS ON THE RIG DRILLED INTO ONE OF THEIR STRUCTURES...
THAT'S AN EXPENSIVE INTUITION!

I KNOW. I'LL DIP INTO MY SAVINGS AND GO ALONE... HELLO? AIR FRANCE?... ONE TICKET ON THE NEXT FLIGHT TO MARTINIQUE, PLEASE...
TWO!!
MAKE THAT THREE!... THERE GOES OUR SAVINGS!

ALL RIGHT... SEE YOU AT THE AIRPORT AT TEN TOMORROW WITH ALL THE EQUIPMENT! I'LL TAKE CARE OF THE TICKETS...
SO MUCH TO DO! WE WON'T SLEEP TONIGHT!
YOU WILL ON THE PLANE!
4A

22 HOURS LATER...
WE'VE STARTED OUR DESCENT TO MARTINIQUE... LANDING IN 15 MINUTES... TEMPERATURE IS 65º... PLEASE EXTINGUISH YOUR CIGARETTES AND FASTEN YOUR SEAT BELTS...
PAUL, WAKE UP!
AIR FRANCE

HEY...PAUL!
WAAAAAAH...
SSHHHH!

3:30 P.M., LOCAL TIME. THE 747 LANDS AT LAMENTIN, MARTINIQUE AIRPORT...
WHAT A WAY TO WAKE ME! GREAT! NOW I HAVE A HEADACHE!
AIR FRANCE
PAAWWW
WHIIIIUUUUUUUUU
4B

FORT-DE-FRANCE
AIR FRANCE
WHHH

LET'S CHECK OUR LUGGAGE AND FIND THE OFFICE OF THE DRILLING COMPANY.
...NEED AN ASPIRIN
WE DON'T EVEN KNOW THE NAME !...

THE COMPANY'S CALLED "FOREX". THEY'VE BEEN ALL OVER THE NEWS LATELY. THEY'RE BASED IN ST-PIERRE. YOU'LL FIND THEM THERE.
THANKS !
...GOT SOME ASPIRIN ?
AIRLINE

LATER, OUTSIDE THE TERMINAL...
CAN YOU TAKE US TO ST-PIERRE ?
SURE !

1 HOUR LATER, IN ST-PIERRE DE LA MARTINIQUE...
THE FOREX COMPANY, PLEASE ?

FOREX ?... ACROSS TOWN... SECOND ROAD TO THE LEFT... THERE'S A SIGN...
TAXI

SOON.
KEEP THE CHANGE...
THANK YOU ! ENJOY YOUR VACATION !
VACATION ?
IELL-FOREX
20
TAXI

SHELL-FOREX
HOPE THEY'VE GOT ASPIRIN !
LOOKS LIKE SOMETHING'S GOING ON HERE !

REPORTERS ?!... TV !... OH, BOY ! THIS IS GOING TO BE FUN!... WHY DON'T YOU TALK TO MR. FREEMAN, THE DRILL ENGINEER... HE'S INSIDE...
HEY, BOSS ! TV PEOPLE !... AND THERE'S A GIRL !

TV ? A LADY ? NO WAY ! I'VE GOT ENOUGH PROBLEMS !
MR. FREEMAN ?
TRITON TWO TO TRITON THREE... OVER !

I JUST WANT TO SHOW YOU THIS GLAZED, LUMINOUS AND MAGNETIC SPHERE !...
?

YOU EXPECT ME TO BELIEVE THAT THIS BALL AND THE STUFF WE DRILLED INTO ARE ONE AND THE SAME ?!!!
I'D LOVE FOR YOU TO PROVE ME WRONG ! LET'S COMPARE THEM !

THAT'S EXACTLY WHAT WE'LL DO ! I'VE HAD ENOUGH OF ALL THIS !... THE LARGER PIECES ARE IN FORT-DE-FRANCE FOR ANALYSIS... BUT THESE SHOULD DO...

TAKE YOUR PICK !
WATCH...

?
POK PLOK
POK

VIC, WHAT DO YOU THINK ?
SAME THING YOU DO... THE FRAGMENTS AND THE SPHERE HAVE AN IDENTICAL TEXTURE !
THIS IS MIND-BOGGLING ! THE MAGNETIC STRENGTH IS SO POWERFUL, I CAN BARELY PULL THE PIECES OFF... WHERE DID YOU GET THIS ?

THAT DOESN'T MATTER NOW !... ALL YOU NEED TO KNOW IS THAT YOUR PLATFORM IS IN DANGER !...
I KNOW ! A STORM IS FORCING US TO EVACUATE !
A STORM ?

YES ! I CAN'T FIGURE IT OUT ! HUGE WAVES ARE SURROUNDING THE PLATFORM INSIDE A 7-MILE RADIUS AND THREATEN TO TOPPLE IT...
THE CHOPPER'S ANSWERING ! HE'S IN SIGHT OF THE COAST !

COME WITH ME ! WE'LL HAVE THE LATEST NEWS !
WHAT ? YOU MEAN YOU DON'T HAVE RADIO CONTACT WITH THE RIG ?...
VRRRRR

FOREX
-TBK
IMPOSSIBLE ! EVERYTHING'S SCRAMBLED WHERE THE PHENOMENON'S TAKING PLACE...

STEVE!? ALONE? WHERE ARE MEL AND HARRY?
THEY STAYED ON BOARD!... A STRANGE DEVICE GOT STUCK BETWEEN THE BEAMS OF THE RIG... SEEMS THERE'S A WOUNDED MAN INSIDE... THEY'RE TRYING TO GET HIM OUT... BUT THERE'S A SNAG...
FOREX
?

THE GUY'S STUCK IN A TRANSLUSCENT BUBBLE... BUT WE CAN'T OPEN IT, OR DRILL A HOLE! IT'S TOO HARD!... I CAME TO GET THE LASER-SAW AND ITS OPERATOR!
LASER-SAW?
OH, MY! HE'S NOT HERE!

HEY! I KNOW HOW TO OPERATE IT! I'LL GO WITH YOU!...
WOW! WHO'S THIS GIRL?

TV PEOPLE!
RIGHT! ANYTHING FOR A JUICY SCOOP! FORGET IT...

...WHERE I GO THERE'S NO ROOM FOR AN EXOTIC BIRD... EVEN AS PRETTY AS YOU!!

OK, ENOUGH OF THIS! LOAD THE LASER! I'M GOING BACK!
ALL RIGHT!
EXOTIC BIRD? ME?

10 MINUTES LATER, THE LOADED CHOPPER TAKES OFF...
HOLD MY PURSE! QUICK!
WHAT ARE YOU DOING?
?
7A

FLY!
YOKO!

NO!

!
?
STOP!

THE PILOT DIDN'T SEE HER! HE'S PICKING UP SPEED!
CALL HIM ON THE RADIO! QUICK!

FOREX
WOW! HE'S GOING FULL SPEED! HOPE THEY'LL LET HIM KNOW FAST!...

STEVE! SLOW DOWN!... THE GIRL IS HANGING ON YOUR LEFT FLOAT!...
WHAT?!!
7B

THE PILOT QUICKLY HOVERS IN PLACE...
I CAN SEE HER... HEY! HOLD IT!...
FOREX

ARE YOU NUTS!... YOU COULD HAVE WAITED FOR ME TO LAND!...
STEVE! WHAT IS SHE DOING?
WASTE OF TIME!

NO, FREEMAN! I'M NOT COMING BACK! THIS GIRL'S GOT GUTS... AND IF SHE REALLY KNOWS HOW TO USE THE LASER...
YOU WANT PROOF? THEN HURRY UP!
?!!

20 MINUTES LATER...
THIS IS WHERE THE SWELLS START... THE SUPPLY SHIP EVACUATED ALL THE PERSONNEL AND IS WAITING FOR AN IMPROVEMENT IN CONDITIONS TO GET BACK TO THE PLATFORM... UP AHEAD ON THE HORIZON!
!
FOREX

SOME OF THE WAVES ARE 30 FEET HIGH... YOU'LL SOON FEEL THEM!

THIS IS HUGE!... IS IT CONNECTED TO THE BOTTOM?
NO! IT'S IMMERSED HALFWAY BY GIGANTIC BALLAST TANKS HOOKED UNDER EACH POD... THEORETICALLY IT CAN'T FEEL THE SWELL... BUT THIS TIME WE'RE WAY BEYOND RED ALERT... AND IF THE ANCHORS BREAK FREE!!...
T3 V
T3 II
T3 I
R.Leloup 88

...AND THEY'LL DISLOCATE THE WHOLE PLATFORM!... ALREADY THERE ARE CRACKS ALL OVER... HERE, IN THE MUD PIPE...

MUD!...

IF WE EMPTY THAT MUD UNDER THE RIG, IT'LL INCREASE THE DENSITY OF THE WATER AND STILL THE WAVES... IF IT FLOATS LONG ENOUGH!...

GREAT IDEA! THAT MUD IS A MIX OF OIL AND BENTONITE*... YOU'RE A GENIUS!... BUT WE DON'T HAVE ENOUGH MANPOWER TO DO IT!

* BENTONITE: CLAY POWDER.

WE'RE FIVE WITH THE GUY IN THE WATER... THE CHOPPER CAN LIFT SEVEN... LEAVE THE LASER HERE AND GET TWO MORE MEN!...

OK!

MY TWO FRIENDS! THEY'RE WORTH A DOZEN!...

READY WHENEVER YOU ARE, MEL...
!
HARRY'S IN POSITION IN THE CRANE... GOOD!! YOU, RED, COME WITH ME!...

DID YOU UNDERSTAND HOW TO DO IT?
YEAH!
GO AHEAD THEN! OPEN THE FIRST VALVE!
2
1

IMMEDIATELY THE PIPE SPURTS THICK LIQUID...

...SPRAYING THE WAVES AND STILLING THEM...
THE SWELL IS STILL STRONG ... THE BASKET WILL HAVE TO FOLLOW ITS MOVEMENTS ... GUIDE THE CRANE, STEVE! LET'S DO IT!!
OK, MISS!

WE'RE MOVING TOO MUCH! I CAN'T OPERATE THE LASER FROM HERE! ONLY ONE SOLUTION!

YOKO!
10 A

THE LASER KNIFE, VIC! GIVE ME MAXIMUM LIGHT INTENSITY. I'M AFRAID THE BEAM WILL DISPERSE IN THE GLASS!...

IT'S FOGGY INSIDE... AT LEAST IT'S A SIGN HE MAY STILL BE ALIVE!!...

AFTER 5 LONG MINUTES...
IS HE ALIVE?
I CAN'T TELL. HE'S IN A DIVING SUIT... THAT REMINDS ME...
HEY!

THIS BOX ATTACHED TO HIS THIGH!... THIS TIME...

NO DOUBT ABOUT IT! IT IS...

JUST THEN, A POWERFUL WAVE CRASHES THROUGH THE OILY MASS, AND...
WATCH OUT!!
R. Leloup
10B

HOIST!!
WAIT!

YOKO!

I WAS JUST ABOUT TO DROP HIM WHEN HIS AIR TUBES SNAPPED! GEE, IT'S TOUGH TO REMOVE THIS HELMET... HERE!... THE MOMENT OF TRUTH...

ASPHYXIATED! HE'S ALL BLUE!

BLUE, YES! DEAD, I'M NOT SURE!
THERE'S A STETHOSCOPE IN THE FIRST-AID UNIT... WE'LL BE ABLE TO CHECK QUICKLY!...
11A

SOON...
HE'S ALIVE!... BUT HIS BREATHING IS VERY WEAK... MORE LIKE A RATTLE... HIS RIB CAGE MUST HAVE BEEN BROKEN... WE HAVE TO GET HIM ASHORE!
DON'T BOTHER! NO DOCTOR COULD SAVE HIM...

THIS MAN IS A VINAN... ONLY HIS PEOPLE CAN DO SOMETHING FOR HIM...
A VINAN?! WHAT IN THE WORLD IS THAT?...

BLUE-SKINNED MEN AND WOMEN WHO ABANDONED THEIR DOOMED PLANET AND TOOK REFUGE ON EARTH SOME 400,000 YEARS AGO... OR RATHER, INSIDE THE EARTH WHERE, IN A STATE OF CONTROLLED LETHARGY, THEIR BIOLOGICAL SYSTEMS ARE BEING ADJUSTED SO AS TO LIVE ON THE SURFACE SOME DAY...
SAY MISS, ARE YOU PULLING MY LEG?
LISTEN!

THERE! LOOK!...
WHHIIIIIIIII

NOW, HONORABLE DOUBTERS...

YOU CAN'T DENY THE EVIDENCE... VIC, WASN'T I RIGHT? WE WERE SUPPOSED TO SEE THEM AGAIN HERE...
I ONLY HOPE THAT THIS REUNION IS GOING TO TAKE PLACE THE WAY YOU FORESEE IT!
11B

WHHiiiiiiiiiii
?
HE'S CHANGING COURSE! HE'S TRYING TO TELL US SOMETHING... VIC! WHERE ARE THE TRANSMITTERS?
IN THE HELICOPTER!
GET THEM!
FOREX

HE KEEPS CIRCLING AT THE SAME ALTITUDE...
SOMETHING'S BOTHERING HIM...

WHAT ARE YOU GOING TO DO?

COMMUNICATE BY THOUGHT, ASSUMING THIS DEVICE IS STILL WORKING...
?

YOKO HAD BARELY PUT THE TRANSMITTER ON WHEN A CLEAR IMAGE CAME THROUGH
WHHiiiiiiiii
!
THE... CHOPPER IS IN THE WAY... QUICK! MOVE IT ASIDE!...

LET THEM LAND... I'M READY FOR THEM!
!?

ARE YOU NUTS?... YOU SHOULD HAVE LEFT THIS WITH THE WOUNDED... YOU'RE SUPPOSED TO BE WATCHING HIM...
OH, YEAH? AND WHAT IF THE GUY WOKE UP AND WANTED TO USE IT?... IT'S A DEVASTATING WEAPON!!...

AS SOON AS STEVE MOVED THE CHOPPER, THE MYSTERIOUS SHIP DESCENDED VERTICALLY...
TRITON 3

...AND LANDED ON THE PLATFORM
PLEASE... KEEP YOUR COOL!
TRITON 3

IF YOUR INTENTIONS ARE AS PURE AS YOUR THOUGHTS, EARTHLING, HAND OVER WHAT YOU'RE HIDING BEHIND YOUR BACK!
CALM DOWN, VINKA!...

YOKO COULDN'T HURT ANYONE!
KANI!!

I AM SO HAPPY... I WAS SO AFRAID THAT I WOULD NEVER SEE YOU AGAIN... HEY, WHY THE LONG FACE?... AREN'T YOU HAPPY, TOO?
OF COURSE I AM, YOKO! BUT I DON'T FEEL LIKE SMILING WHEN I KNOW THAT YOU ARE IN MORTAL DANGER!

MORTAL DANGER?!!
YES!... WHEN THEY DRILLED IN THE GROUND, THESE MEN DESTROYED ONE OF OUR PIPELINES AND TRIGGERED A CATACLYSM WHICH IS GOING TO KILL YOU FIRST IF YOU STAY HERE!...
WHAT IS SHE SAYING?

WHAT WAS THERE IN THAT PIPELINE?
LAVA! OR TO BE MORE PRECISE, MOLTEN MAGMA!

LAVA! UNDER AN OIL LAYER!
WHAT?!

LAVA IN THIS SPOT! IT IS GEOLOGICALLY IMPOSSIBLE!
THEY BROUGHT IT HERE... ONLY I DON'T KNOW FOR WHAT PURPOSE!
COME WITH ME, YOKO. I'LL SHOW YOU!
GOOD GOD! NOW I UNDERSTAND!...

THE PRESSURE HAS BEEN CLIMBING HOURLY IN THE THREE WELLS ALREADY SUNK... THE HYDROCARBONS HEATED BY THE LAVA TURN QUICKLY INTO GASES... AND THE GRANITE LAYER SEPARATING THEM IS ONLY 700 FEET THICK!
IT'LL COLLAPSE... AND THE EXPLOSIVE GASES WILL REACH THE LAVA!
13A

THE APOCALYPTIC SCENE TAKES SHAPE IN YOKO'S MIND...
THE EXPLOSION WILL BE HUGE... A GIGANTIC TIDAL WAVE WILL CRASH ON MARTINIQUE... THE SHOCK WAVE COULD ACTIVATE MOUNT PELEE, WHICH KILLED 30,000 PEOPLE IN 1902...
NO!

YOU HAVE CONTROL OVER THE FORCES OF NATURE, YOU MUST PREVENT THIS FROM HAPPENING!
WE DO HAVE A PLAN, YOKO... BUT WE'RE STILL MISSING ONE ELEMENT TO SUCCEED...

THAT ELEMENT IS... YOU!
ME?!! HOW COULD I HELP, REALLY!?

I'LL TELL YOU LATER IF YOU WANT TO FOLLOW ME. I MUST WARN YOU, THOUGH, THAT YOUR LIFE IS AT RISK!
WHAT'S MY LIFE COMPARED TO THOUSANDS OF OTHERS... I'M GOING!
WE'RE ALL GOING!
13B

WHILE THE VINANS BOARD THE WOUNDED, YOKO GIVES HER LAST INSTRUCTIONS...
KANI SAYS THAT THE SWELL OF THE WATER WILL STOP AS SOON AS WE SUCCEED... GIVE US 24 HOURS...
ALL RIGHT! BUT AFTER THAT, WE'RE ALERTING EVERYONE!

HALF AN HOUR LATER, AS THE SUN VANISHES ON THE HORIZON...
WHIIIIIIII

WHIIIIIIIIIII
YOKO! DO YOU HAVE THE SPHERE?

SURE! HERE! IS IT IMPORTANT?
AS MUCH AS YOU! BOTH HAVE A ROLE TO PLAY!
WE'RE HEADING FOR MORE TROUBLE!
14A

BEEP... APROACHING LANDING ZONE...
WATCH OUT! OUR SEATS WILL ROTATE...
?

...WE'RE SWITCHING TO VERTICAL MODE!
HEY!
WHIIIIIII

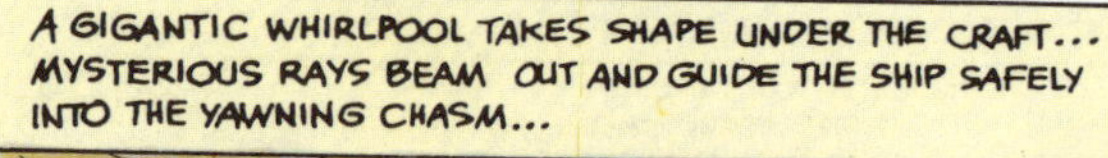
A GIGANTIC WHIRLPOOL TAKES SHAPE UNDER THE CRAFT... MYSTERIOUS RAYS BEAM OUT AND GUIDE THE SHIP SAFELY INTO THE YAWNING CHASM...

PAUL! DON'T MOVE! IT'S OK!
OK? WE'RE FALLING BACKWARD...

...INTO THE SEA!!
WHIIIIIII

WHIIIIIIII
R Leloup 14B

80 FEET DOWN, THE LIQUID TUNNEL IS REPLACED BY A VERTICAL TUBE...
KANI, IF THIS IS A RETRACTABLE TUBE, WHY NOT BRING IT ALL THE WAY TO THE SURFACE?

BECAUSE OF THE STORM! THAT WHIRLPOOL IS NECESSARY TO BREAK THE WAVES AND MAINTAIN THE STABILITY OF THE TUBE THROUGH ITS GYROSCOPIC EFFECT!

THE CRAFT MAKES IT THROUGH THE LOCK CHAMBER OF THE WELL AND DESCENDS AT GREAT SPEED INSIDE THE EARTH CRUST...
WE HAVE ALMOST LEFT THE HYDROCARBON LAYER... AND NOW, YOKO, WATCH!
?
WHHH

OH! THAT GLOW! COULD THAT BE...?
THE LAVA, YES!

IT IS SLOWLY INFILTRATING EVERY CRACK... BUT THERE'S NO DANGER TO THE TUBE. IT'S PERFECTLY ISOLATED AND COOLED!

WHAT ABOUT THE GAS PRESSURE?..
IT WILL HOLD!... WELL, WE HOPE IT WILL...
BEEP..

CAREFUL! FINAL PHASE!...

THE CRAFT SLOWS DOWN AND HOOKS ITSELF TO A STRANGE CRADLE...
WHHH

...WHICH TIPS IT INTO HORIZONTAL POSITION AS SOON AS THE ENGINES ARE TURNED OFF...
KANI, I HAVE A QUESTION: WHAT ABOUT AIR?!

IT'S SIMILAR TO WHAT YOU BREATHE ON THE SURFACE, AND IS ACTUALLY PARTIALLY FUNNELED THROUGH THE WELL WE JUST USED!
R Leloup

ALL SET ?
YES, BUT... THERE ARE THREE

CAN'T SEPARATE THEM... NEVER MIND, THESE BOYS ARE GOING TO HELP US PUT OUR PLAN INTO ACTION!... WHERE ARE "THEY"?
"THEY" ARE WAITING FOR YOU NEAR THE GENERATOR!

VIC AND PAUL, STAY HERE! YOKO, COME WITH ME!...
?

LIKE IT OR NOT, YOU HEARD THE LADY!
OK! OK!...
HURRY, YOKO!

THIS IS LANA, AND HERE'S SILKA... TWO TRUSTY FRIENDS! ... I DON'T NEED TO INTRODUCE YOU TO THE THIRD ONE!
POKY!!
YOKO!
16A

YOKO IS BACK! YOKO IS BACK! YOKO IS...
LANA RESEMBLES YOU MOST... WE DYED AND CUT HER HAIR... YOU ARE GOING TO TRADE IDENTITIES BY EXCHANGING YOUR CLOTHES...
WHAT ABOUT HER BLUE SKIN?...

OUR TV MONITORS ARE MONOCHROMATIC... ACTUALLY, WE ARE BEING TRACKED THROUGH THE MAGNETIC I.D. IN OUR BELTS... KANI AND SILKA WILL ALSO EXCHANGE THEIRS...
WAIT! I DON'T HAVE ANY I.D. TO EXCHANGE!!
YOU HAVE MUCH BETTER, YOKO!

YOUR SPHERE! THANKS TO ITS RADIATION, I WAS ABLE TO LOCATE YOU ON THE SURFACE... TO FIND OUT YOUR DESTINATION AND TO WAIT FOR YOU THERE!...
UNDER SURVEILLANCE! WITHOUT KNOWING IT!...

5 MINUTES LATER, THE YOUNG WOMEN JOIN VIC AND PAUL...
GOOD! EVEN PAUL BOUGHT IT!
WAAAAH! SHE TURNED BLUE!
?
NEAT! MY FRIEND GRUMPY IS HERE, TOO!

YOU SCARED ME... ALTHOUGH I MUST ADMIT, YOUR BLUE VERSION IS EXQUISITE!...
GOOD. YOU'LL HAVE PLENTY OF TIME TO ADMIRE HER BECAUSE YOU AND VIC WILL GO WITH THEM IN ORDER TO REMAIN UNCONSPICUOUS, KANI AND I MUST FINISH THEIR ASSIGNMENT... AND THAT'S AN ORDER!...

SOON, KANI TOOK YOKO TO A STEEL-PLATED DOOR PROTECTED BY A BEAM OF LIGHT...
THIS BEAM CONTROLS THE DOOR. IF IT IDENTIFIES YOU AS LANA, IT WILL OPEN...
LET'S TRY THEN!
16B

YOKO STEPS UP AND INTERRUPTS THE BEAM...

IN A FEW SECONDS, THE HEAVY DOOR OPENS...
ASPIRING VINAN SUNO'S APPLICATION IS ACCEPTED!...

AND IT LOOKS LIKE MY FRIENDLY LOOK-ALIKE HAS SUCCESSFULLY PASSED HER TEST, TOO!
SSHHHH! KEEP IT LOW!

VOICES CARRY FAR IN THESE CAVES, AND WITHOUT A TRANSLATOR, YOUR VOICE DOESN'T SOUND VINAN AT ALL!
17A

LOOK WHO'S THERE! THE KING'S DAUGHTERS WAVE GOODBYE TO THEIR VALIANT KNIGHTS...
BYE-BYE!
PERFECT! WE COULDN'T DREAM OF BEING MORE DISCRETE!
PAUL! KEEP QUIET!

I AM AFRAID WE'RE QUICKLY GOING TO BE VERY POPULAR! WHO ARE THOSE TWO?...
THOSE...? OH!!
?

THIS WAY! QUICK!
HEY! YOU TWO!

THEY WENT INSIDE!
I WANT TO KNOW WHY THEY RAN... STAY HERE IN CASE THEY TRY TO GO AROUND US!
UP THERE!

R. Leloup.

WHAT NOW?...
THE PIPES. THEY'RE OUR LAST CHANCE!
17B

WATCH OUT! IT'S SLIPPERY!

ALL OF A SUDDEN, ONE OF THE PIPES SLIPS AND...
YOKO!

OOOH!

HE'S COMING THIS WAY! WHAT DO WE DO?

TRY THE NEXT LEVEL!
STOP!
18A

HE'LL TAKE THE NEXT ELEVATOR AFTER US...
!

I KNEW IT! WE HAVE TO GET RID OF HIM AT THE TOP, OR ELSE!...

FINALLY, THE NEXT LEVEL...
HEY! THIS IS PERFECT FOR...
FOR?...

YOKO!? WHAT...
WHERE'S THE OTHER ONE?

WOOooow!
SPLAF
18B

THIS TYPE OF EXPLOSION PUT OUR COMMUNITY AT GREAT RISK, AND WE DECIDED TO REVEAL OUR EXISTENCE TO THE EARTHLINGS, AND IMPOSE OUR RIGHT TO LIVE ON THE SURFACE...

BUT KNOWING THAT NO GOVERNMENT WOULD GIVE US LAND, WE RESOLVED TO USE AN EXTENSION OF THE EARTH CRUST TO CREATE A NEW CONTINENT!

WITH LAVA ?!!...

WITH THIS LAVA, WE ACTIVATED AND MONITORED AN OLD VOLCANO... OUR GOAL WAS TO CREATE AN ARTIFICIAL ISLAND WHICH WOULD BE THE FIRST STEP TO THE FUTURE VINAN CONTINENT...
THAT'S INSANE!

NO, MERELY A SPECTACULAR WAY TO IMPRESS EARTHLINGS WITH OUR TECHNOLOGY AND DISCOURAGE A VIOLENT REACTION!...
HERE'S THE LAVA!...

I ASSUME THESE ARE THE PIPELINES?...
YES, AND HERE TRAGEDY STRUCK... AS YOU WILL SEE...
20A

KANI STOPS THE CRAFT...
BEFORE CLIMBING UP THERE, LET'S TAKE SOME PRECAUTIONS...

PUT ON THIS HOOD, IT WILL PROTECT YOUR EYES FROM THE INTENSE GLARE OF THE LAVA!

WHAT... THIS PIPE HAS BEEN CUT OFF!
NO! IT MELTED!
R. Leloup
20B

LATER...
MIND-BOGGLING!
THE VIEW ABOVE THE THIRD PIPE WILL SURPRISE YOU EVEN MORE!

SEE THE OTHER SIDE, WHAT'S LEFT OF IT!

THE MEN ON THE OIL RIG COULDN'T HAVE CAUSED SUCH DAMAGE ?!!
UNFORTUNATELY, THEY HAVE! THE DRILL BIT HIT THE PIPELINE IN THE GRANITE AND DESTROYED THE THERMAL REGULATION BETWEEN TWO RELAY STATIONS... THE SECTION BECAME DISTORTED AND MELTED, FREEING THE LAVA ...

...TO POUR INTO THIS FAULT CHAMBER WHICH AT ITS LOWEST POINT LIES BELOW THE SALT DOME CONTAINING THE HYDROCARBONS!
AND THAT'S WHERE YOU THINK THE WALL SEPARATING OIL AND GAS WILL GIVE IN ?...

NO DOUBT ABOUT IT!... AND UNDER THE MAGNITUDE OF SUCH AN EXPLOSION, THIS FAULT COULD STRETCH ALL THE WAY TO THE EARTH MAGMA ...
21A

AND JUST HOW COULD I PREVENT THAT ?
SIMPLY BY CLOSING THE VALVE TO THIS PIPELINE!

WHY HAVEN'T YOU DONE IT YET ?
KARPAN OPPOSES IT... HE WANTS THIS DISASTER... A TIDAL WAVE WOULD ELIMINATE THE INHABITANTS ON SURROUNDING ISLANDS... AND THEN NOTHING COULD STOP HIM FROM SEIZING THEM!

THAT'S RIDICULOUS. PEOPLE WOULD UNITE TO GET RID OF HIM. TWO OR THREE NUCLEAR BOMBS AND...
...AND KARPAN WOULD RETALIATE WITH SUBTERRANEAN THERMAL EXPLOSIONS. HE CAN LOWER ENTIRE LANDS BELOW SEA LEVEL ...

...OR AWAKEN INACTIVE VOLCANOES... SPEAKING OF VOLCANOES ...

...THIS ONE SAW THE BIRTH OF LIFE ON EARTH!
!
21B

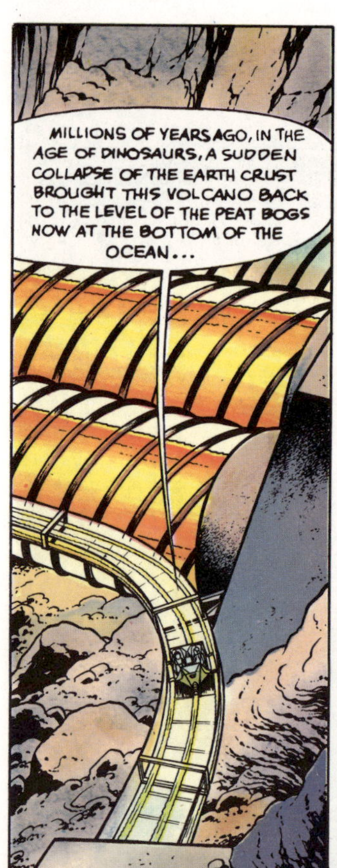
MILLIONS OF YEARS AGO, IN THE AGE OF DINOSAURS, A SUDDEN COLLAPSE OF THE EARTH CRUST BROUGHT THIS VOLCANO BACK TO THE LEVEL OF THE PEAT BOGS NOW AT THE BOTTOM OF THE OCEAN...

SINCE ITS SHAFT WAS NOT FED ANY MORE, THE LAVA IT CONTAINED HARDENED... IT IS THIS LAVA CORK THAT WE ARE PUSHING BACK UP TO THE SURFACE OF THE SEA!
BY PUMPING FRESH LAVA UNDER IT FROM ANOTHER PLACE?
EXACTLY!

YOU CAN SEE FOR YOURSELF! PUT YOUR HOOD ON... AND IF SOMEONE TALKS TO YOU... DON'T ANSWER!

THE LAVA, BROUGHT HERE IN THE PIPELINES, IS INJECTED UNDER PRESSURE INTO THE SHAFT OF THE VOLCANO...
!
22A

THE ENERGY USED IS ENORMOUS AND THE WHOLE OPERATION IS REMOTE-CONTROLLED!

MORE FIREPROOF BULKHEADS!...
THE WHOLE AREA IS RINGED WITH THEM... WISE PRECAUTION!

THIS PLACE IS UNDER MAXIMUM SURVEILLANCE... LET'S MAKE IT SHORT!
!

BUT YOKO IS STUNNED BY THE UNEXPECTED SIGHT...
THE BOTTOM OF THE OCEAN!!...
SSHHH!!
22B

SO THAT'S THE LAVA CORK ! IT'S HUGE !!
ON THIS SCREEN, WE CAN SEE IT WITHOUT ALL THE STEAM CREATED BY THE CONTACT OF LAVA WITH WATER...

BUT THEN, CAN'T THE WATER TRICKLE INTO THE SHAFT AND CAUSE IT TO EXPLODE !!?
NOT A CHANCE. THE PRESSURE FROM THE LAVA IS SO STRONG THAT IT EXPANDS INTO THE SEA !
?
LET'S GO NOW !

BUT YOKO CAN'T PULL HERSELF FROM THE ENTHRALLING VIEW ON THE LARGE SCREEN...
THAT'S THE SAME CRAFT AS THE ONE ON THE OIL RIG !... WHAT WAS FLOATING WAS ONLY THE COCKPIT !...
?

WHAT'S WITH HER ? NEVER SEEN ANYTHING LIKE THIS BEFORE ?!...
ERR !!... SHE'S NEW IN THIS UNIT !!...
DARN ! THE USUAL PAIN-IN-THE-NECK !

A NEW FACE !... THAT'S TOO RARE TO PASS UP !...
OUCH !!

AN EARTHLING !
BRUTE !
23A

ALERT !!...

?

AAAAAH

BLONK

THERE ! TWO GIRLS RUNNING ! BLOCK ALL THE EXITS !!
QUICK ! YOKO !!
?

TOO LATE !
VLAMM
23B

WITHOUT HESITATION, KANI DRAWS HER DISINTEGRATOR
HOLD THEM! BUT WATCH IT! SOME OF THEM ARE ARMED!...
GOT IT!

BACK OFF, SOLDIERS!

READY, YOKO!!...

ONCE THROUGH...
BRROMM
THEY'RE CLOSING THE OUTSIDE DOORS!
?

THIS WAY! IT'S OUR ONLY CHANCE!

EVERYTHING'S DESTROYED IN THIS SECTOR!...
NO! IT'S JUST BEEN EXCAVATED! NOTHING'S CONSTRUCTED YET!

HURRY! THEY'RE RIGHT BEHIND US!
OUR ONLY HOPE IS RIGHT THERE!...

...IF THEY LEAVE US ENOUGH TIME TO GRAB IT!
24B

I'LL HOLD THEM OFF! GET THE MACHINE!...
!

WATCH OUT!

YOKO WON'T BE ABLE TO STOP THEM FOR LONG. GOT TO HURRY...

...BEFORE SOMEONE UP THERE NOTICES US...

GOOD, HE'S ALONE!

IF YOU WANT TO LIVE... GET OUT OF HERE, REAL FAST!
25A

MEANWHILE, IN THE TUNNEL...
AIM FOR THE VAULT, ABOVE HER!...

!

BOM

DZZZZZ

KANI DID IT!
TIIIUUW

SCRASH
25B

YOKO, COME HERE! TAKE MY PLACE IN THE LASER COCKPIT... I'LL DRIVE THIS DEMOLISHER OUT!
O.K.!

UNDERSTAND ?!... LEFT HANDLE RAISES THE DOME... RIGHT FOR ROTATION AND FIRING...
A CHILD COULD DO IT!...

KANI JUMPS INTO THE OTHER SEAT...
THEY CUT THE POWER, BUT WE HAVE ENOUGH IN THE ACCUMULATORS TO FORCE OUR WAY THROUGH...

SLIDING ON A MAGNETIC CUSHION, KANI GUIDES THE DEMOLISHER INTO THE FINISHED PART OF THE SECTOR...
THERE'S THE DOOR... GO AHEAD, YOKO! A LITTLE BLAST TO CHASE AWAY THESE IDIOTS WHO WANT TO STOP US... AND THEN FULL POWER, FROM THE BOTTOM UP...

I DON'T MEAN TO HURT THEM!...
26A

YOKO BLASTS A LARGE BREACH IN THE DOOR, AND KANI DRIVES THE MACHINE...
THEY CLOSED THE PIPE LOCK CHAMBERS, AND WE DON'T HAVE ENOUGH POWER LEFT TO PIERCE THEM!...
THEY'RE OPENING ONE ON THE LEFT!...

AS THE DEMOLISHER REACHES THE PIPE, A NEWCOMER EMERGES FROM IT AT LOW SPEED...
THAT'S KARPAN'S MAGNETOCARRIER! YOKO, SHOOT THE PROPELLERS! BLOCK HIM IN THE CHAMBER!...

BANZAI!
TIIIUUUWW
R. Leloup 26B

WE CAN'T MOVE! ALL THE PROPELLER CIRCUITS ARE DESTROYED!...
LOWER THE LADDER! I WANT TO TALK TO THESE FOOLS!

VRRRRRRRRR
!
THE ESCAPE HATCH! QUICK!!

HEY!! THEY'RE NUTS!

O.K., KANI! WHAT DO WE DO NEXT?
ABANDON THE DEMOLISHER... COME! MAYBE WE CAN MAKE IT!...
FEMALES!

THE EARTHLING! HERE?... KANI BETRAYED US!!...

...AND NONE OF THOSE DUMMIES TRIES TO STOP THEM! CALL THEM!
I CAN'T. ALL THE CIRCUITS ARE DOWN!
27A

RUNNING UNDER THE MAGNETOCARRIER, KANI GUIDES YOKO INSIDE THE TUBE...
YOU WANT TO ESCAPE THROUGH THE TUBE?... ON FOOT?!...

WHO SAYS WE'RE WALKING?
VLAM
WHAT IN...?

EMERGENCY SLEDS... IN CASE OF A BREAKDOWN IN A TUBE... QUICK! UNHOOK YOURS!

BY THE DEVIL! THEY'RE ESCAPING!
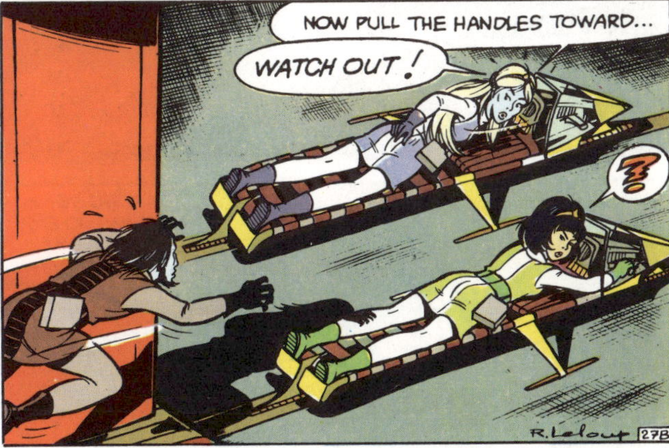
NOW PULL THE HANDLES TOWARD...
WATCH OUT!
?!
R. Leloup
27B

PAF
THE HANDLES, YOKO! PULL !!!...

AS KARPAN BITES THE DUST, YOKO IMITATES KANI AND PULLS THE HANDLES OF THE SLED, IMMEDIATELY JUMPING FORWARD!...

YOU HIT?...
NO! JUST A FEW BURNT HAIRS!!...

THERE ARE OTHER SLEDS!... WHAT ARE YOU WAITING FOR?!! I WANT TO KNOW WHERE THEY'RE GOING!!...
THEY'RE ALREADY FAR AWAY!!

AND YOU'LL PAY FOR ABANDONING THE DEMOLISHER!...
HEY! MY JOB IS DIGGING TUNNELS... YOU HANDLE SECURITY... AND WE KNOW HOW WELL YOU'VE DONE THAT!!

CAREFUL, WE'RE GOING TO ANOTHER LEVEL!...
?
28A
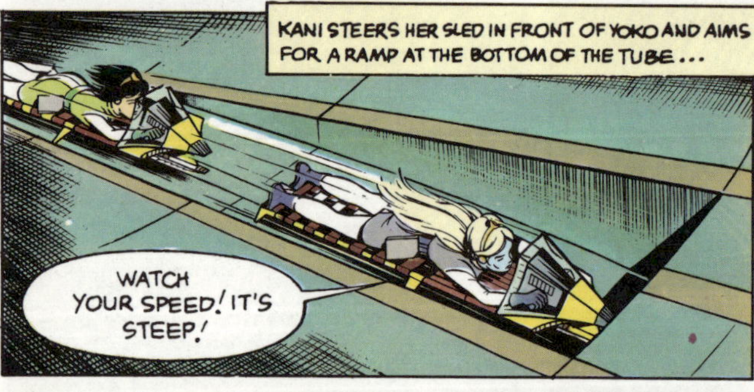
KANI STEERS HER SLED IN FRONT OF YOKO AND AIMS FOR A RAMP AT THE BOTTOM OF THE TUBE...
WATCH YOUR SPEED! IT'S STEEP!

WOW! THE LOWER WE GET... THE HIGHER MY STOMACH CLIMBS!

THIS TOBOGGAN SLIDE HAS NO END! AH! LIGHT AHEAD!

THE END OF THE TUBE AND, FOR YOKO, THE BEGINNING OF A STUNNING DISCOVERY...
!?
GIANT MUSHROOMS!!...
28B

MUCH TO YOKO'S SURPRISE, KANI STOPS HER SLED IN THE MIDDLE OF THE STRANGE VEGETATION...
WHY STOP HERE? THE SMELL OF THIS MUSHROOM FOREST IS TERRIBLE!!
NO CHOICE! WE HAVE TO GO THROUGH IT!

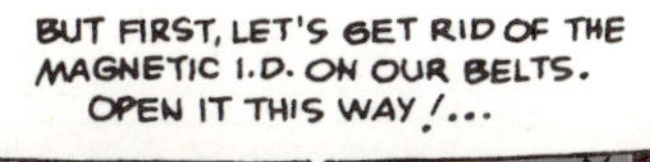
BUT FIRST, LET'S GET RID OF THE MAGNETIC I.D. ON OUR BELTS. OPEN IT THIS WAY!...

KLING

THAT WAY THEY'LL HAVE A HARD TIME LOCATING US... COME!

LATER...
STAYING WOULD HAVE BEEN SUICIDAL! KARPAN MOST LIKELY SOUNDED THE ALARM...
THE LAVA PIPE LINES! NO WONDER IT'S LIKE A SAUNA HERE!
29A

RIGHT! THIS ENVIRONMENT IS SIMILAR TO THE CAVES ON OUR PLANET AND SO WE TRIED GERMINATING SPORES WE HAD BROUGHT WITH US.

EXTRATERRESTRIAL PLANTS! I KNEW IT!... AND WHAT'S THE PURPOSE IN GROWING THEM?
MEDICINAL... AND SENTIMENTAL... IT REMINDS US OF OUR DEFUNCT PLANET...

WE'RE NEARING THE SPOT WHERE VIC AND PAUL SHOULD BE WAITING FOR US...
THIS IS THE KIND OF PLACE THAT DRIVES PAUL CRAZY!... WE'RE GOING TO HAVE FUN!...

I THINK YOU MAY HAVE UNDERESTIMATED HIM!...
OH!

PAUL!
HE'S FOUND A VINAN SOLUTION TO HIS GRUMPINESS!
HI THERE! DID YOU ENJOY THE WALK?
YOKO! AT LAST!
R. Leloup
29B

DON'T TELL ME YOU BROUGHT THIS ANIMAL, TOO?
NO, THIS ONE'S BEEN HERE AWHILE!
SECONDARY ERA... CRETACEOUS PERIOD TYRANOSAURUS...
TALK OF STEALING OTHER PEOPLE'S LINES!...

MOMENTS LATER, VIC WAS BRIEFED...
...WE HOPED TO GET KARPAN OUT OF THE WAY... AND WE'VE DONE THE EXACT OPPOSITE...
WHERE ARE THE TWO GIRLS WHO PLAYED OUR ROLES?
THEY WENT AHEAD WITH THE MAGNETIC CARRIER AFTER LEAVING US IN THE HANDS OF THESE YOUTH!

WE ONLY HAVE TWO SOLUTIONS!... EITHER WE FORCE OUR WAY THROUGH TO BRING YOU BACK TO THE SURFACE... OR WE TRY TO REACH THE LAVA FLOW CONTROL SECTOR...
THE SECOND ONE! UNANIMOUSLY!
WHAT?!...

BUCKLE UP IN FRONT OF THESE YOUNG LADIES... AND INFORM YOUR TENDER HEART THAT THE OLDEST IS ONLY FOURTEEN!
PFF! YOU GET OLD QUICKLY AT THAT AGE!
FOURTEEN AND A HALF!

GET BACK TO YOUR UNITS AT ONCE!... TOO LONG AN ABSENCE MIGHT RAISE SUSPICIONS...
HE WANTS US TO GO INTO THE BEAST!!
?
30A

THIS CARCASS AND HUNDREDS OF OTHERS HAVE CREATED A MULTITUDE OF ROUTES IN THIS LAYER OF CLAY, THROUGH WHICH WE WILL REACH OUR GOAL: THE FLOW CONTROL SECTOR!
ARE YOU SURE THEY'RE ALL DEAD?

THIS WILL GIVE LIGHT; HOOK IT TO YOUR BELT...
WAIT! THIS DOESN'T HAVE A LAMP!

THE BOX EMITS WAVES OF ENERGY WHICH CAUSE FLUORESCENCE IN A SUBSTANCE WE SPRAYED ON THE WALLS...
LET'S GO! KARPAN CAN'T BE FAR BEHIND!

INDEED, AT THE OTHER END OF THE MUSHROOM FOREST...
WE DON'T HAVE ENOUGH MEN AND EQUIPMENT TO DIG IN THERE!
OK! I'LL GO BACK TO THE FLOW CONTROL SECTOR AND SEND MEN WITH DETECTORS... THEN I WILL PERSONNALLY MAKE SPECIAL ARRANGEMENTS!...

WE LEAVE THE BACK OF ONE ANIMAL AND ENTER THE FRONT OF ANOTHER!... I CAN'T MAKE HEADS OR TAILS OF THIS EXPEDITION!...
30B

SOON THE PATH LEADS DOWN...
THIS PART IS THE MOST PRECARIOUS!

...TO THE BOTTOM OF A WIDE POCKET...
WE HAD TO STOP DIGGING THIS TUNNEL BECAUSE THE ROCKS WERE CATCHING FIRE UNDER THE DISINTEGRATORS...
NO WONDER, IT'S COAL!

SINCE THE TUNNEL IS PLUGGED, WE DUG A PASSAGEWAY ALONG THE EDGE...
AND WHERE DOES IT LEAD?..

DIRECTLY INTO THE LAVA FLOW SEC...
POKY! NO!!... NOT THAT WAY!
31A

COME HERE, ALL OF YOU! MY FRIENDS THE EARTHLINGS ARE HERE!
POKY, COME!
EARTHLINGS!?
WHERE?
!
?

ALL RIGHT! I'LL SHOW YOU A FEMALE EARTHLING, BUT KEEP QUIET!

IN A SECOND...
WHY ISN'T YOUR SKIN BLUE?
OH! LOOK HOW BLACK HER HAIR IS!
DON'T SPEAK SO LOUD!

WHAT'S THIS ALL ABOUT!! WHAT!? THE EARTHLING!... HERE!...
?
!

AAAAAAH
?!
RLeloup.
31B

LONG AGO, WE USED THESE PROJECTILES ON EARTH ANIMALS, BUT NEVER AGAINST MAN!

THAT'S CHANGED NOW!...

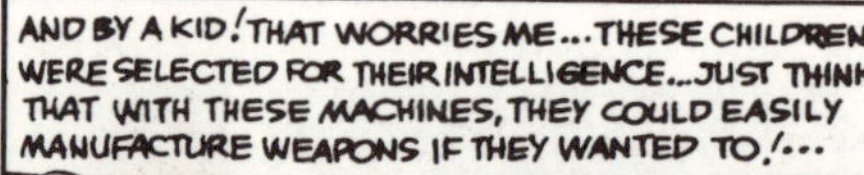

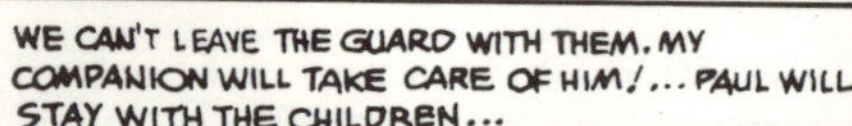

THIS IS WERE THE LAVA, AFTER BEING FILTERED AND PURIFIED, IS DISTRIBUTED TO THE PIPES!

32B

LET ME SEE IF I'M RIGHT, KANI... THE COILS AROUND THE PIPES CREATE A MAGNETIC FIELD... WHICH MOVES THE LAVA... AND THIS SET OF CABLES ENERGIZES THE SPIRALS...

I KNOW WHAT YOU'RE THINKING, YOKO: CUT THE CABLES!... BUT THAT WOULD TAKE TOO MUCH TIME. THE CIRCUITS HAVE BEEN TRIPLED... AND THEY WOULD SPOT US BEFORE WE COULD REACH THEM!...

...AND ALSO IF WE STAY HERE!... LET'S CHECK THE FILTERS!...
THE FILTERS?

YES, BEFORE THE LAVA IS SENT TO THE PIPELINES, IT'S FILTERED AND CLEANED OF GASES AND SLAG...

THERE! THE FILTERS!
WHAT A FURNACE!!
33A

THEY GET CLOGGED QUICKLY AND NEED TO BE CLEANED FREQUENTLY ABOVE THAT BASIN...

...ALL THE IMPURITIES ARE THEN DISINTEGRATED INTO MOLECULES AND THEN RECOMBINED WITH THE LAVA...

33B
SAY, KANI, CAN THAT SUSPENDED CARRIER ACCESS THE FLOW CONTROL SECTOR?
YES!!! WHAT'S YOUR PLAN?
?

* In Mythology, Goddess of Hunting.

** God of the Forges and the working of Metals.

LATER, NEAR THE FILTERS...
GIVE ME A MINUTE ALONE! I NEED TO CONCENTRATE!...

I HAVEN'T PRACTICED KYUDO* IN A LONG TIME.

QUIETLY, YOKO AIMS...

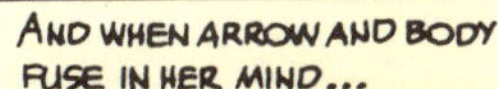
* Japanese Archery

AND WHEN ARROW AND BODY FUSE IN HER MIND...

I DID IT!
ARGH!

THE "COMMANDO" UNIT QUICKLY REACHES THE PLATFORM...

HURRY! THEY'RE HOISTING THE LAST FILTER!...

HERE'S THE TRACK... ALL WE NEED IS TO CONNECT THE BACK-UP CIRCUITS... IF WE HAVE ENOUGH TIME!...

VIC, GIVE ME A HAND! YOKO, WHERE ARE THEY WITH THE FILTER?
THEY'RE MOVING IT TO THE BASIN... WE'RE GOING TO MISS IT!...

OH, NO!! THAT WOULD BE TOO STUPID!
YOKO!
TCHAK

DON'T DO IT ALONE!
35B

THERE! A MAINTENANCE HATCH!

IT'S OPEN! GOT TO GO!

AAAAH...
36A

MEANWHILE ABOVE THE SUPPORT TRACK...
THE CABIN STOPPED. DID SHE SUCCEED?

YOKO! I'LL NEVER QUITE UNDERSTAND YOU!
I'D SAY IT'S THIS GUY WHO DOESN'T QUITE UNDERSTAND WHAT'S GOING ON! HE DIDN'T RESIST AT ALL!

HE DOESN'T BELONG TO KARPAN'S UNIT! HE MIGHT EVEN SIDE WITH US IF WE EXPLAINED, BUT WE DON'T HAVE TIME! VIC, KEEP AN EYE ON HIM!
O.K.!

A MINUTE LATER...
AS I RECALL, THE RIGHT HANDLE CONTROLS MOVEMENT!...
THE MORE YOU LEAVE TO YOUR MAGNETIC MEMORY, THE MORE YOU'RE BOUND TO LOSE YOUR OWN!

KANI BRINGS THE CABIN BACK TO THE TRACK LEADING TO THE FLOW CONTROL SECTOR...
NOW, FULL SPEED AHEAD!
HURRY! THERE'S A LOT OF ACTION BELOW!

INDEED, BELOW...
FILTER COMMAND TO CENTRAL COMMAND... SOMETHING IS GOING ON... SOME STRANGERS TOOK CONTROL OF THE SUSPENDED CARRIER AND ARE NOW HEADING TOWARD THE FLOW SECTOR! ...
36B

AT CENTRAL COMMAND, IN THE FLOW SECTOR...
WHAT? THEY'RE HEADING IN THIS DIRECTION? WITH A FILTER!! WHO?
WE SPOTTED TWO GIRLS AND A GUY!
WHAT?! CUT THE TRACK POWER!
?

DONE!... BUT IT IS STILL FUNCTIONING. THEY'VE CONNECTED THE EMERGENCY CIRCUITS!

THOSE DARN GIRLS! WHAT'S BEHIND THIS? I HAD ALL THE MAGNETIC CONTROLS DOUBLED AND MEN POSTED AT EVERY ENTRY!

WHY DON'T YOU ASK THEM?... AND THEN ASK WHAT THEY INTEND TO DO WITH THE TORCH THEY'RE BRINGING?!!
HERE THEY ARE!

YOKO, LET'S TRY TO NEGOCIATE!
SURE! WE HAVE A WEIGHTY ARGUMENT! ... HE BETTER NOT REFUSE!...
37A

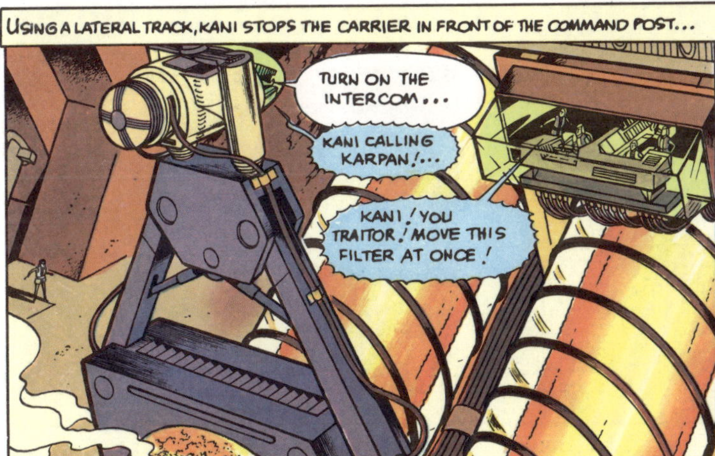
USING A LATERAL TRACK, KANI STOPS THE CARRIER IN FRONT OF THE COMMAND POST...
TURN ON THE INTERCOM...
KANI CALLING KARPAN!...
KANI! YOU TRAITOR! MOVE THIS FILTER AT ONCE!

ONLY IF YOU STOP POURING LAVA INTO PIPE THREE... OR WE'LL PUT IT OUT OF COMMISSION BY DROPPING THE FILTER ON THE CIRCUITS!...
WELL PUT! HE MUST BE GOING NUTS!

THAT WOULDN'T CHANGE ANYTHING! ACCORDING TO OUR LATEST DATA, THE OCEAN FLOOR WILL GIVE IN IN 48 HOURS... YOU'D NEED TWICE THAT TO COOL AND HARDEN THE LAVA IN THE CREVICE!

YOU IDIOT! IT'S THE WALL BETWEEN THE LAVA AND THE HYDROCARBONS THAT IS GOING TO GIVE IN! AND WE'RE GOING TO BE THE FIRST VICTIMS OF THIS DISASTER! YOUR INSANITY'S BLINDING YOU KARPAN!
ENOUGH OF THIS! GET OUT!
SO THE THIRD PIPE DOESN'T BOTHER HIM!... HOW ABOUT THE OTHER TWO?...

... RIGHT BELOW US!
KANI, HOW DO YOU CONTROL THE TONGS?
HERE, THIS ONE!

YOKO GRABS THE LEVER AND PRESSES IT FIRMLY DOWN...
YOKO! NO!!
WITH GREETINGS FROM YOKO SUNO!
KLAK
37B

THE TONGS OPEN AND THE FILTER...

...CRASHES DOWN ON THE CENTRAL PIPE...
KRAAK

FROM WICH THE LAVA, NO LONGER CONTROLLED BY THE MAGNETIC FIELD, SPLASHES OUT...
38A

WHAT HAVE YOU DONE?!! THE WHOLE STRUCTURE WILL BE DESTROYED IF...IF...
IF THEY DON'T SHUT DOWN THE LAVA FLOW! OUR METHODS MAY BE DIFFERENT, BUT THE RESULT IS THE SAME!

PIPE 2 IS OUT AND THE CIRCUITS OF THE OTHERS ARE ON FIRE ... HEY! WHAT ARE YOU DOING?!...
I'M GOING TO TRAP THEM LIKE RATS!

THE FIRE BULKHEADS!! YOU'RE INSANE!... SOME OF OUR MEN ARE DOWN THERE!
BROOM

NOW CUT THE AIR SUPPLY IN THERE AND OPEN THE SMOKE VENTS...
STOP! YOU'RE GOING TO ASPHYXIATE OUR OWN PEOPLE!...

IF HE FREES THOSE SULFUROUS GASES, WE'RE ALL DOOMED!!
THERE'S ONLY ONE WAY TO STOP HIM! MOVE ASIDE!

ALL RIGHT! WE TRUST YOU!...
NOW IS THE TIME... THEY'RE FIGHTING!
LEAVE ME ALONE, FOOL! AAAH!... YOU ASKED FOR IT!...
AAAAH!
38B

THAT'S WHAT THEY CAN ALL EXPECT!
AAAAAH

NOW LET'S TAKE CARE OF THE OTHERS!...
KARPAN, YOU'RE MAD!!

ALL OF A SUDDEN, A SINISTER NOISE STOPS KARPAN...
KRRR
?

KRRAAAK
!
!
WATCH OUT!

SCRASH
AAAAAH
39A

NOW PULL BACK!
STOP! A MAN IS STUCK IN THE DEBRIS!... OOH! IT'S KARPAN!

IGNORING KANI'S CRY, THE VINAN PILOT MERCILESSLY OPENS THE GIANT TONGS, AND...
AAAAAH

WHAT A HORRIBLE DEATH!
HE FELL INTO THE LAVA!

IT WAS HIM OR US!... THE VINAN PEOPLE HAVE PUT UP LONG ENOUGH WITH THIS MONSTER... HE DIVIDED US... A PITY HIS DEATH WILL NOT PREVENT THE CATACLYSM...
39B

LOOK BELOW! THE LAVA'S COVERING EVERYTHING!
!
TURN THE COCKPIT!

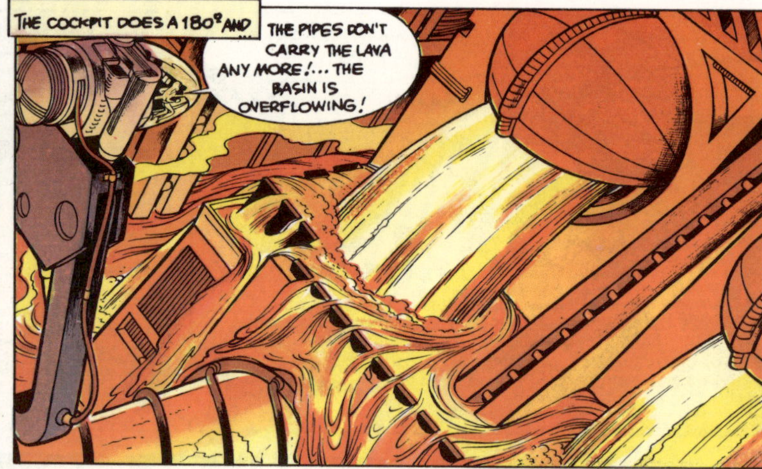
THE COCKPIT DOES A 180° AND ...
THE PIPES DON'T CARRY THE LAVA ANY MORE!... THE BASIN IS OVERFLOWING!

AS LONG AS THE LAVA DOESN'T REACH THE CIRCUITS OF THE CENTRAL BLOCK, THE FLOW WILL CONTINUE!... WE MUST EVACUATE THE CHILDREN BEFORE THEY CAN'T BREATHE!
TO THE FILTERS, QUICKLY!

SOON, ABOVE THE FILTERS...
YOU WILL ANSWER FOR YOUR BEHAVIOR!
THAT'S THE GUARD YOU ELECTROCUTED!

THERE'S NO MORE SECURITY! KARPAN IS DEAD!... IF YOU HOPE TO SURVIVE, YOU'D BETTER SWITCH SIDES AND COME WITH US!

TAKING BACK THE SAME PATH, THE SMALL GROUP LEAVES THE FLOW SECTOR FLOODED BY LAVA...
THERE'S ONLY ONE FLOW OPEN, BUT THE LAVA STILL...
IT'S FLOWING BACK THROUGH THE PIPES... SOON EVERYTHING WILL BE FLOODED!

POOR KARPAN! HE DREAMED OF DOMINATING BY FIRE AND BLOOD... THE VERY COLORS OF HIS GRAVE!
COME! THE CHILDREN ARE IN DANGER!

SOON, YOKO IS REUNITED WITH PAUL AND THE VINAN CHILDREN...
HEY! WHAT'S BURNING?
YOU DON'T WANT TO KNOW! WE HAVE TO GET OUT OF HERE!

AFTER A PAINFUL CLIMB BACK UP...
...GLAD TO SEE THIS CUTIE AGAIN!
R. Leloup

WHEN THEY REACH THE BOTTOM OF THE CAVE...
UH-OH! NEWCOMERS MEAN PROBLEMS!
NO! THEY'RE OURS!

BOM
KANI!... THE EARTHLINGS! THE CHILDREN, ALL SAFE! PRAISE THE SUPREME POWER!...
VINKA!

AFTER WHICH TOLD VINKA THE STORY...
KARPAN DID NOT LIE! IN LESS THAN TWO EARTH DAYS, THE WALL IN THE FAULT WILL BREAK! WE NEED THREE DAYS TO COOL THE LAVA... THERE'S ONE SOLUTION, BUT IT'S VERY DANGEROUS TO THE EARTHLINGS!
BE SPECIFIC!

RELEASE THE OVERCOMPRESSED GASES TO THE SURFACE THROUGH THE ACCESS WELL. THAT WAY WE COULD EASE THE PRESSURE AND GAIN THE DAY WE NEED!
THE GASES WILL SPREAD IN THE ATMOSPHERE AND THE SLIGHTEST SPARK COULD IGNITE THEM... BOOM!
UNLESS YOU DO IT THE MOMENT THEY EXIT!

VIC IS RIGHT! WE HAVE TO TRY IT!
VEGA! I KNOW I CAN TRUST YOU! REPLACE KARPAN! EVACUATE THE CHILDREN, THEN TAKE YOUR MEN TO THE GREAT FAULT! I'LL MEET YOU THERE!
IT WILL BE DONE!
41A

MOMENTS LATER, THE MAGNETIC CRAFT TURNS AROUND, TAKING OUR FRIENDS TO THE EXIT TUNNEL...
WHAT ABOUT THE STORM, KANI?
IT'S OVER! PUTTING PIPE 3 OUT STOPPED IT... THE SEA WILL BE CALM BY THE TIME WE REACH THE SURFACE!

2 HOURS LATER... ON THE SURFACE, DAWN ILLUMINATES A CALM CARIBBEAN... AT LAST... ON THE OIL RIG, THE MEN ARE UNDECIDED...
MEL, WHY WON'T YOU LET THE FREIGHTER COME ANY CLOSER?!

BECAUSE OUR INSTRUMENTS ARE CLEAR: THE PRESSURE IS STILL RISING!
LISTEN!
I'M GETTING WORRIED ABOUT YOUR FRIENDS...
WHIIIIIII

HERE THEY COME!

SOON, THE VINAN CRAFT LANDS ON THE PLATFORM...
WHIIIIIIIIIIII
41B

STEVE! GET YOUR CHOPPER READY! MEL, LISTEN TO ME!
?

THE PRESSURE IS INCREDIBLE! THE PILLAR OF FIRE IS GOING TO BE GIGANTIC... AND THE POLLUTION DEVASTATING!
THINK THEN WHAT THE EXPLOSION WOULD BE LIKE!... ENOUGH TALK, LET'S ACT!

LET'S NOT ALL TAKE THE SAME RISK!... TAKE THE CHOPPER... THE CAMERA'S THERE... THERE'LL BE SOME AMAZING SHOTS... WHICH COULD REFILL OUR COFFERS!...
WHY ARE THEY EMPTY IN THE FIRST PLACE?!
HUSH! BE CAREFUL!

YOU CONVINCED THEM?
IT WASN'T EASY!... LET'S PLAY IT SAFE AND LET THE CHOPPER TAKE OFF.

A MINUTE LATER...
FOREX
TRIT
T3 IV
WHIIIIIII
42A

KANI HOVERS JUST ABOVE THE WATER, FACING THE WHIRLPOOL OF THE EXIT WELL...
KANI TO VINKA... STANDING BY... OVER!!...
VINKA TO KANI... STAND-BY... COUNTDOWN PROCEEDING... 3-2-1! IT'S ALL YOURS! GOOD LUCK! OVER AND OUT!
WHIIIIIII

IN A FEW LONG SECONDS... SUDDENLY...
HANG ON YOKO!

THOUSANDS OF CUBIC YARDS OF HYDROCARBON GASES ARE SET ABLAZE INSTANTLY... KANI PULLS OUT AT FULL SPEED AND SHIELDS THE CRAFT FROM THE GIGANTIC BLAST...
WHIIIIIII
R. Leloup 42B

UNDER UNBELIEVABLE PRESSURE, THE PILLAR OF FIRE REACHES AN AMAZING ALTITUDE...
SHOOT, PAUL! SHOOT!
WHAT DO YOU THINK I'M DOING?

WE'VE DONE IT! IN LESS THAN THREE DAYS, THE LAVA WILL HAVE SOLIDIFIED AND THE PRESSURE DROPPED... ALL WE'LL NEED TO DO IS DISMANTLE THE PIPE BY DISLOCATING IT WITH ULTRASOUNDS...
HOW ARE YOU GOING TO JOIN THE OTHER VINANS?

I'LL FLY INTO ORBIT... AND JOIN A BASE LOCATED IN ONE OF YOUR HIGHEST MOUNTAINS, AT AN ALTITUDE TOO HIGH FOR HUMANS...
OH?

...AND WHERE WE ARE PUTTING THE FINISHING TOUCHES ON A PROJECT OPPOSITE TO KARPAN'S: THE RETURN TO OUR UNIVERSE!
TO YOUR PLANET?!!
WHIiiiiii

YES, IF IT SURVIVED AND IS HABITABLE... OTHERWISE, FIND OUR PEOPLE ON THE DIFFERENT WORLDS WHERE THEY MIGRATED LONG AGO... BUT I WILL NEVER LEAVE EARTH...

...WITHOUT SEEING YOU AGAIN... TAKE THIS! IT LOOKS LIKE WHAT YOU CALL TELEVISION...

THE SURVIVAL KIT OF THIS SHIP HAS SEVERAL OF THEM, ALL OPERATIONAL... WHEREVER WE ARE ON EARTH, WE'LL BE ABLE TO SEE EACH OTHER! LET ME TELL YOU HOW TO USE IT... AND THEN WE'LL HAVE TO GO OUR SEPARATE WAYS...

MINUTES LATER...
YOU CAN PULL UP THE DOOR, KANI!

MAY THE SUPREME POWER PROTECT YOU, YOKO! TELL PAUL AND VIC... THAT FLEEING... SOMETIMES MEANS HIDING YOUR TEARS...

KANI OPENS THE ENGINES, AND THE SPACECRAFT BLASTS TO THE SKY...
WHIiiiiiiiiiiiii

?

FOR THREE NIGHTS, THE INFERNAL TORCH BURNS HIGH IN THE CARIBBEAN SKY. THEN THE FLAME STARTS DECREASING HOURLY...
THE PRESSURE KEEPS GOING DOWN...

RIGHT NOW, IT'S BELOW THE LEVEL WE ENCOUNTERED WHEN WE DRILLED... WHAT ARE YOUR "BLUE BIRDS" WAITING FOR ?
WHERE'S YOKO ?
UP THERE ! SHE'S CHIT-CHATTING. IF THERE'S ANYTHING NEW SHE'LL TELL US...
YES, KANI ! AN ENDLESS PARADE OF PLANES TODAY... PRESS, RADIO, TV... ONE AFTER THE OTHER... TRUE TO HIS WORD, MEL DID NOT SAY A PEEP ABOUT YOUR EXISTENCE... BUT HE'S WORRIED... WE'RE EXPECTING AN INQUIRY TOMORROW...

TELL HIM HE HAS NOTHING TO WORRY ABOUT. THE LAVA IS NOW HARD AND VINKA JUST SIGNALED THAT HE'S ABOUT TO DISINTEGRATE THE TUBE... CALL ME BACK WHEN IT'S OVER !
ALL RIGHT !

IT'S ABOUT TIME THEY STOP THIS THING ! THIS FIRE COULD GO FOR YEARS... AND I CAN'T LIE ONE MORE DAY TO THE AUTHORITIES !
LOOK !
?

SUDDENLY, AS IF BLOWN OUT AT ITS BASE, THE BLAZE IS EXTINGUISHED...
...AND GONE... ONLY THICK CLOUDS REMAIN, SLOWLY FADING ABOVE THE SILENT SEA...

PHEW ! NOW I CAN BREATHE EASY !... ALL RIGHT, WE'VE LOST ENOUGH MONEY ! CALL THE FREIGHTER ... BACK TO WORK AT DAWN !...
CALL KANI !
HOW CAN YOU THINK ABOUT MONEY AFTER THIS ?!
LATER, ABOVE THE DERRICK...
YES, YOKO. THE VOLCANIC ISLAND PROJECT IS ABANDONED...
WISE MOVE, KANI ! FATE HAS BROUGHT US TOGETHER TWICE TO FACE THE WORST, BUT MY INTUITION TELLS ME...

...THAT THE THIRD TIME WILL BE... TO BUILD THE BEST !
AND REMEMBER, HER INTUITIONS ARE ALWAYS RIGHT !
YEAH ! EVEN IF THEY COST US A BUNDLE !
THE END
STORY AND ART: R. LELOUP. COLOR: STUDIO LEONARDO.